SPIRIT WITH US

Faith Stories for Young Children

Written by Judith Dunlap
Illustrated by Steve Erspamer, S.M.

ST. ANTHONY MESSENGER PRESS

Cincinnati, Ohio

DEDICATION

For tomorrow's Church, today's children,
especially my grandchildren, Jacob and Nicholas

=====

Nihil Obstat: Rev. Nicholas Lohkamp, O.F.M.
Rev. Edward J. Gratsch
Imprimi Potest: Rev. John Bok, O.F.M.
Imprimatur: Most Reverend Carl K. Moeddel, V.G.
Archdiocese of Cincinnati, May 21, 1997

Illustrations by Steve Erspamer, S.M.
Cover and book design by Sanger & Eby Design
ISBN 0-86716-289-9
Text copyright ©1998, Judith Dunlap
Illustrations copyright ©1998, Steve Erspamer, S.M.
All rights reserved.
Published by St. Anthony Messenger Press
Printed in the U.S.A.

CONTENTS

The Spirit at Work

When God made the world, God had a plan. Everyone and everything would live in peace and harmony. In the Plan of God, people would love God more than anything. They would love others as they loved themselves. But something went wrong. People misused their gift of freedom. They broke God's peace. They forgot about God's love. They forgot that they were supposed to love everybody.

God sent Jesus to remind people about the Plan. God sent Jesus to help people remember the Good News. This is the Good News: God will always love us. God will always be with us.

Jesus was God's Son. When Jesus walked the earth, God was with us in a very special way. Jesus' love was God's love. His hands were God's hands. His voice was God's voice. Jesus did not just tell people the Good News; Jesus was the Good News.

After Jesus died, the Holy Spirit came to be with Jesus' friends. God is still with us in a very special way because the Holy Spirit is with us and in us. Now our love can become God's love. Our hands can become God's hands. Our voices can become God's voice. Together, we become God's people. With the help of the Holy Spirit, we can be the Good News to the world.

God is also with us in a very special way when we receive the sacraments. The sacraments are seven very special gifts. When we receive one of the sacraments, the Church celebrates "God with us" here and now. These are the seven sacraments: Baptism, Confirmation, Eucharist, Penance, Matrimony, Holy Orders and the Sacrament of the Sick. In this book, we will talk about some of these sacraments.

We will also find out how the Church was born. You will find out how our Church celebrates that God is with us and that we are with God. You will hear about people who heard God's call and became the Good News. You will learn to listen for the Holy Spirit in your life.

Church

Sometimes a church is very big.
Sometimes it is quite small.
Sometimes when we say the word,
We don't mean a place at all.

I know that Church can also be
Grown-up folks and kids like me
Who come to pray and worship God
And make God's Plan a reality.

Pentecost: The Day the Spirit Came

A long, long time ago, the apostles, Jesus' mother, Mary, and some other women were together celebrating the Jewish feast of Pentecost. They went to the same room where they had celebrated the Passover with Jesus. It was hard for the apostles to believe that seven weeks had passed since their last supper with Jesus.

They spent a lot of time together after Jesus ascended into heaven. They prayed and they talked. They liked to share stories about Jesus. They liked to say, "Remember when...." They also worried about what would become of them now that Jesus was gone.

The apostles wanted to do what Jesus had told them. They wanted to share the Good News with others. But they just did not know how they could do this. Jesus' friends had so many questions. They had all seen Jesus after he had risen. They had all

been with Jesus when he returned to heaven. They just did not know what to do next.

Jerusalem was crowded. People from all over the world were there to celebrate the feast of Pentecost. Jesus' friends were glad to be together in the Upper Room. They were glad that they had a place to come to pray. They prayed for each other. They prayed for their families. They prayed that they would be able to do everything Jesus had asked them to do.

Suddenly, they heard a great noise. It sounded like a roaring wind. The noise filled the whole house. The apostles looked around to see what was making the sound. In front of them, they saw what looked like tongues of fire. They should have been afraid, but they were not.

The tongues of fire came to rest on each of their heads. The fire did not feel hot. It did not burn their hair. Yet inside their hearts they began to feel the power of the wind. Inside their hearts, they began to feel the warmth of the fire.

They were all filled with the Holy Spirit. When they opened their mouths to talk, they began to speak in different languages. This really surprised them. They had never been outside of Palestine. They did not even know anyone who could speak another language. Yet here they were, talking in whole sentences to each other in strange languages. They were so excited they began to shout. They ran out of the room and down the stairs. They ran outside into the street.

They were so loud that a crowd began to gather. The people in the streets stopped and stared at them. A man said to his friend, "That man over there looks like a fisherman, but he is talking in Latin." The

other man said, "They all look like they come from Galilee, but this one here is talking in Egyptian." It was true. People from Asia, people from Libya, people from all over the world heard the apostles speaking in their own languages.

Peter stood up in front of everyone. He began to talk about Jesus. He told them how Jesus had died and risen from the dead. He reminded them that the

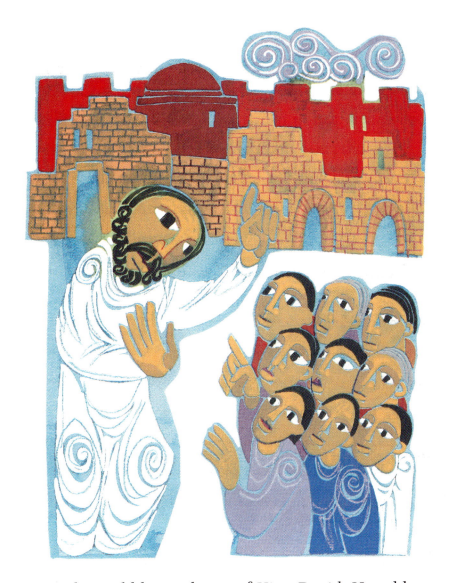

Messiah would be a relative of King David. He told
them Jesus was this promised Messiah.

Many, many people listened to Peter. They wanted
to know more about Jesus. Peter told them they
would have to be sorry for their sins. He told them
they would have to be baptized. When they were

baptized, they would receive the gift of the Holy
Spirit. Many of those people became believers.

Now Jesus had many more followers. The Holy
Spirit showed the apostles what they must do. The
Holy Spirit filled them with the power to share the
Good News. People who had never met Jesus came to
believe in Jesus' message. Pentecost became the
birthday of the Church.

God called out to the people gathered. The people
listened and answered. The great and Holy Spirit was
not only with them but also in them. And when they let
the Spirit move them, great things began to happen.

Spirit of Belonging

It feels great to belong! It feels comfortable. It feels safe. It feels right. It is especially good to belong to our Church. It is like being a part of a great big family. We take care of each other. We help each other. We celebrate with each other.

The people in our Church are all different, just as in regular families. We like different things. Some people like loud music. Some people like soft music. Sometimes we even speak different languages. But that is all right because our Church is still one big family.

Our Church is one family because we all have the same Creator, God, and the same Brother, Jesus. We also share the same great and Holy Spirit. It is the Spirit that makes us one.

Jesus promised his friends before he died that God would send the Spirit. Jesus promised that the Spirit would be with us. Jesus promised that the Spirit would be in us. Through the power of the Holy Spirit, great things can happen. Together, through the Holy Spirit, we can begin to make the Plan of God happen.

The way we become members of our Church family is through the Sacrament of Baptism. That is why we call Baptism the sacrament of belonging. In the Sacrament of Baptism we receive the great and Holy Spirit.

In the stories that follow, you will hear about two people who wanted to become members of our Church family. One person heard about Jesus and believed. He was baptized right away. The other person believed in Jesus, but had to wait a long time before being baptized. The important thing is, they both received the sacrament of belonging and great things happened.

Philip and the Ethiopian

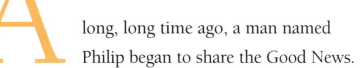

A long, long time ago, a man named Philip began to share the Good News. Philip was a Jew who spoke Greek. As the early Church got bigger and bigger, the apostles realized they could not do everything themselves. They told the believers to choose seven people to help them. Philip was one of those chosen.

Philip liked to tell people about Jesus. He told them what Jesus said. He told them what Jesus did. He told them how Jesus died on the cross and rose from the dead. Philip did such a good job talking about Jesus that many Jews came to believe that Jesus was the Messiah.

One day, an angel spoke to Philip. The angel told Philip to get ready to leave by noon. The angel told him to set out on the road from Jerusalem to Gaza. Philip knew that this road went right through the desert. He knew that it would be very hot walking down the road at noon. Philip went anyway. He trusted God's messenger.

As he walked down the road, Philip noticed a fancy chariot. (A chariot was a special wagon in

which rich people rode.) Philip could tell by the decorations that this chariot came from a faraway land. The Holy Spirit told Philip to go and walk along beside the fancy chariot.

The chariot belonged to a man from Ethiopia. Ethiopia is in Africa. The man who owned the chariot was a very important man. He worked for a queen. He took care of all of her money.

The Ethiopian was on his way home. He had been in Jerusalem to worship. He had also gone there to learn more about God. He liked to read the Jewish holy books. He was reading one of them when Philip began to walk beside his chariot.

In those days, people liked to read out loud. It was another way of praying to God. These are some of the words the Ethiopian was reading when Philip joined him:

"He has been humiliated and has no one to defend him.
Who will ever talk about his descendants,
Since his life on earth has been cut short!"

Philip said to the Ethiopian, "Do you understand what you are reading?" The Ethiopian answered, "How can I, unless someone helps me?" Then he

invited Philip to ride
in his chariot with
him.

They rode
together for a long
time. Philip began to
talk about the words
that the man had
been reading.

He explained
all about the
Good News of
Jesus to him.
Finally, he told
him how people
had made fun of Jesus before they killed him. He told
the man how young Jesus was when he died.

As they traveled down the road, they came to a
lake. The man told Philip that he wanted to be a
follower of Jesus. He told Philip he wanted to be
baptized. So they stopped the chariot, and they both
got out. Philip and the man both went into the water.
Philip baptized the Ethiopian. After they came out of
the water, Philip left the man.

Philip went to many different towns and baptized a great number of people. The Ethiopian took his new faith all the way back to Africa. The Church was growing beyond Palestine. Now even people from other lands believed in the Good News.

God called both Philip and the Ethiopian. They both listened, and they both answered. The great and Holy Spirit was not just with Philip and not just with the Ethiopian, but also in them. Philip and the Ethiopian let the Spirit move them and great things happened.

The Maiden Who Finally Came Home

A long time ago, there lived a young girl named Tekakwitha. Tekakwitha was born in North America about a hundred years before Benjamin Franklin and George Washington were born. She belonged to the Mohawk tribe. Her father was the chief.

Tekakwitha's mother belonged to a tribe that was at war with the Mohawks. When she was a young woman, she was captured. Tekakwitha's mother was so beautiful that the Mohawk chief decided he would marry her. Life was not easy for Tekakwitha's mother. She was a Christian and the Mohawks did not like Christians. Her happiest day was when Tekakwitha was born.

Tekakwitha was a beautiful child. She had shining black hair, sparkling brown eyes and dark olive skin. She was also beautiful on the inside. She was kind and good. She would help anyone who needed help. She liked to run and play with the other children. She liked to plant and gather the crops with her mother. She loved to listen to her mother sing lullabies to her baby brother. But Tekakwitha's favorite time of day was evening. After the sun went down, her mother would tuck her in her blankets and tell her stories about Jesus.

When Tekakwitha was four years old her whole life changed. A terrible sickness called smallpox

began to attack the people in her village. Every day more and more people died. Before very long, Tekakwitha's whole family became sick. Within a few days her father and mother and her baby brother all died. Tekakwitha was sick for a long, long time, but the smallpox did not kill her. Instead she was scarred for the rest of her life. Her beautiful olive-skinned face was covered with deep pox marks. Her sparkling brown eyes could no longer see clearly.

It was a very sad time for Tekakwitha. Her uncle, who was the new chief, took her into his family. Tekakwitha worked very hard for her aunt and uncle. She gathered firewood and cooked. Tekakwitha spent most of her time alone. She could no longer see well enough to play with the rest of the children. She liked to remember the stories her mother told her. "Someday," she thought, "I would like the holy water to be poured on me. I would like to be a Christian just like my mother."

When Tekakwitha was a teenager, a Blackrobe (that is what the tribe called priests) came into the village. When Tekakwitha had a chance, she asked him to baptize her. "First," said the good priest, "you must ask your uncle if it is all right."

Tekakwitha was afraid. She knew that her uncle did not like Christians. She prayed and prayed that she would be brave enough to ask her uncle's permission. She prayed and prayed that he would say yes.

The next day she asked her uncle if she could become a Christian. "If you have the water poured, Tekakwitha, life will not be easy for you," he said, "but I will not stop you."

Tekakwitha was so happy! She had loved Jesus for a very long time. Now she would be able to call herself one of his followers. She could not wait— but that is just what she had to do. A whole year passed as Tekakwitha got ready for her baptism. Tekakwitha prayed and listened to the teachings of the Blackrobes.

Finally, the day came. On Easter morning, April 18, 1676, Tekakwitha became a Christian. Tekakwitha took another name when she was baptized. Her Christian name was Kateri. Now she had two names, Kateri Tekakwitha.

Kateri's uncle had been right. Life became very difficult for her. No one would talk to her. When she walked to church on Sunday, people threw stones at

her. After many months of such treatment, the priests became afraid for Kateri's safety. They told Kateri about a village on the other side of the river. The people in this village were of many different tribes, but they were all Catholics. Kateri wanted with all her heart to go to this village.

Kateri knew that her uncle would never let her leave. She would have to sneak out of the village. Finally, the priests decided on a plan to help her escape.

In the middle of the night, when everything was ready, Kateri crept out of her hut. Two friends were waiting to help her escape. They had to be very careful as they went through the forest. Finally, they came to the river. In a short time they were on the other side.

do something wrong and tell God we are sorry, that is prayer. When we say "Alleluia! God is good," that is prayer.

Prayer is when we read stories about Jesus and think about him. Or sometimes we do not have to think or say anything at all. Prayer can just be listening. Sometimes prayer can happen when we are just sitting and watching television after a long day of doing our best. Prayer can be spoken out loud or just thoughts in our head. Prayer can be straight from our hearts without words or thoughts at all. Prayer can be sung and prayer can be danced. Prayer is any time we spend with God.

Sometimes we pray alone and sometimes we pray with other people. Our biggest and best prayer is the Eucharist or the Mass. It is a very special time when God is with us. It is a very special time for us to spend with God.

During the Mass we get to spend time with God in all the ways we have been talking about. We have time to pray alone. And we have lots of time to pray with others. During the Mass we hear about Jesus and the Good News. We even have quiet time to think about Jesus. During the Mass we remember

Jesus in a most special way when the bread and wine becomes Jesus' Body and Blood. During the Mass there is time just to be quiet and listen. And there is time to pray out loud with our brothers and sisters in our Church family.

During the Mass we tell God we are sorry for the things we have done wrong. We ask God for the things that we need. We say, "God is good!" in lots of different ways. And we say "thank you." Did you know that *Eucharist* is the Greek word for "thank you"?

Prayer is a very important part of a Christian's life. It is how we say yes to God, who is always reaching out to us.

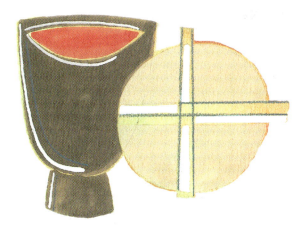

The Church That Began at Home

Along, long time ago, there lived a good Christian woman named Nympha. Nympha lived during the time of Jesus. She lived in a land hundreds of miles away from Jerusalem in a town called Colossae. Nympha had never met Jesus, but she knew all about him.

Nympha learned about Jesus from one of his disciples. After Jesus died, the disciple traveled to her country and told the people about Jesus. He told the people the Good News. He told the people how Jesus had died and had risen from the dead.

Some people just laughed at the disciple, but others listened and became believers. Nympha and everyone who lived in her house were baptized. They worked very hard to make the Plan of God happen.

Nympha had a special gift. She knew how to give great parties. People always felt comfortable when they came to her house. People would come for dinner and stay late into the evening. Everything about Nympha and her home said "Welcome!"

When Nympha became a Christian, her parties were even better. She would invite her Christian friends for dinner, and always they would stay late into the evening. Every week they came to her home for a very special dinner. This is how it went.

"Is everything ready?" Nympha asked.

"Yes," said her servant. "The meat is cooked, the vegetables are ready and the bread is baking."

"Just in time," said Nympha. "Here come our first guests."

The people began to gather in small groups, chatting and laughing. Sometimes Nympha could hear a few people arguing about whose turn it was to read Paul's letter. She also noticed that some people

seemed to be avoiding other people. "Oh my," she thought, "it is a good thing it is almost time to begin the supper."

They began as they always did with a prayer and a song. During the dinner people shared their favorite stories of Jesus. "I like the story about Jesus and Zacchaeus," said one of the guests. He told the others how Jesus had changed the tax collector's life. Everyone laughed when he described how fast Zacchaeus had slid down the tree when Jesus had called him. "I hear old Zack is collecting money for the widows in Jerusalem now," said another woman.

When the story of Zacchaeus was finished, Nympha took the latest letter from Paul out of her pocket. She turned to the man sitting next to her. "Would you please read Paul's letter?" she asked.

The man read the letter nice and loud. "What a good letter," Nympha thought. "It is almost as if Paul is with us tonight." Nympha really liked the part where Paul told them how much God loves them, and asked them to be kind and humble, gentle and patient with each other. She was also glad Paul reminded them to forgive each other as soon as a quarrel began, telling them to remember that God

was always ready to forgive them. As always, Paul
told them to let peace live in their hearts.

After the letter was read, it was time to pray again. Then the servant brought out the freshly baked bread and a pitcher of wine. The bread was prayed over and broken. The wine was blessed and poured. And everyone who was baptized shared in the Lord's Supper. They knew that Jesus was with them. They knew that Jesus was in them. And they knew that through Jesus all things were possible.

As they left the table, they began to sing again. Nympha was happy as she walked her friends to the door. She knew that they had their problems. They had their faults. But she also knew that they loved each other. They were one family.

It is the same today when we gather for the Lord's Supper. We come to pray together as a family. When we receive the Body of Christ at Communion we remember that we are the Body of Christ in this world. And we know that with Jesus, in Jesus and through Jesus all things are possible.

God called Nympha. Nympha listened and Nympha answered. The great and Holy Spirit was not just with Nympha but also in Nympha. Nympha let the Spirit move her and great things happened.

The Woman Who Laughed With God

Not so very long ago, there lived a wonderful, joyful woman named Thea Bowman. Thea liked to talk about God. She liked to sing about God. Thea was a great talker and a great singer. People loved to hear her talk and sing about God. Thea had many, many friends because she was such a happy and loving person. But Thea's best friend was God.

Thea was born in 1937 in Mississippi. Her father worked very hard. He was the only African American doctor in the town. Thea's mother was a teacher and a good woman who helped everyone. Thea's grandfather had once been a slave.

Thea lived during a time when African Americans were often treated badly. But Thea's parents were both loving people. They taught Thea not to return hate for hate. Thea's mother would say, "Hate will just eat into your soul." Thea learned how much God loved her from her parents and from the people in her neighborhood, especially the "old folks."

When Thea was growing up she spent a lot of time with the elders in her neighborhood. Her parents wanted her to learn the old songs and old stories. They wanted her to hear from the elders' lips about slavery and what they had lived through.

The elders taught Thea lessons she would remember all her life. They taught her to be thankful and joyful during the good times. They also taught her to be thankful and joyful in the not-so-good times. Thea would tell people, "The old folks taught me how to face life and pain and even death."

When Thea was ten years old, some Catholic sisters came to her town. They opened up a school for all of the children. Thea liked going to the school. She liked learning how to read. She liked learning more about Jesus. She liked being with the sisters. Thea was a happy, active child. She liked to run and play. She liked to laugh and sing. She liked to learn and pray.

After a while Thea decided she wanted to become a Catholic. Thea's parents gave their permission, and Thea joined the Church. Thea liked to spend time with the Catholic sisters. She liked to help them as they worked for the poor.

After high school Thea decided she wanted to give her whole life to God in a special way by becoming a nun. She wanted to become a Catholic sister just like the sisters who had taught her. And that is just what she did.

Thea left the South and traveled to Wisconsin to learn more about God and the sisters. Sister Thea went to college to learn how to be a teacher. She traveled to a university in Washington, D.C., to learn all about English literature.

Sister Thea loved to learn and she loved to teach. But it was not teaching English literature that made her famous. People all over the world came to know

Thea when she began to write and teach about the music and the history of her people.

Everywhere Sister Thea traveled, she taught people to respect the gifts African Americans have to

offer our country and our Church. She also taught all people to respect their own heritage. Thea used to say, "No matter who you are or what your background, always remember to be proud because you can say, 'I am a child of God. I am somebody.'"

Sister Thea had many talents. She was very smart. She was a great teacher. She was a powerful singer. When Sister Thea sang, she would get everyone to sing. Sister Thea would clap and get everyone to clap. Sister Thea also had a special talent of making people feel good about themselves. She kept telling people, "Always remember who you are and whose you are."

Sister Thea had friends of every race and color. She had friends from all different countries and of all different religions. Sister Thea had so many friends you could not even count them. But Thea's best friend was always Jesus.

Sister Thea prayed all the time. She liked praying at Mass. She liked praying every day with the sisters with whom she lived. She liked to pray when she was alone in her room. She liked to pray with the thousands of people who came to hear her speak. Sister Thea and God were so close that Thea's whole life was a prayer.

In 1984, Sister Thea learned she had cancer. The doctors told her she only had a little while to live. Thea remembered what the old folks had taught her: "Even when you are scared, you got to keep on 'steppin.'" And that is what Thea did. Even when she was in great pain, she would still talk and sing about the God she loved so much.

Hundreds and thousands of people would come to see Sister Thea and hear her. She would look tiny and weak as her wheelchair was lifted onto the platform. But then something wonderful would happen. As soon as Sister Thea began to sing, she became filled with great strength and power. Even when she spoke in a whisper, everyone could hear. Sister Thea was filled with the Spirit of God, and she shared that Spirit with everyone who heard her.

On March 30, 1990, Thea Bowman died. Now she is singing and talking with the God she loved to laugh with all her life.

All through Thea's life, God called to her and Thea answered. The great and Holy Spirit was not just with Thea but also in Thea. Sister Thea let the Spirit move her and great things happened. Sister Thea's singing and celebration of life were her ways of praying. By getting other people of all races and cultures to sing and celebrate their lives, she taught them to pray, too.

Spirit of Forgiveness

Nobody is perfect. Everybody makes mistakes. Sometimes we even hurt other people. And sometimes we are hurt by others. The important thing about making mistakes and doing hurtful things is how we behave afterwards. Do we run and hide? Do we make things worse by telling a lie? Do we say, "It wasn't me"? It takes a lot of courage to say "I did it. I am sorry."

Sometimes when people hurt us with mean and angry words, we want to yell back with even meaner words. We want to get even. We want to make them hurt. When people hurt us, it is hard to forgive them. It is hard to say, "It's OK. Let's start over."

When we hurt others or others hurt us, we need to take a deep breath, count to ten and ask God for help. With the help of the Holy Spirit we can find the words to say, "I'm sorry" or "I forgive you." It is not easy, but with God's help we can do it.

In our Church we have a special sacrament of forgiveness. It is called the Sacrament of Penance or Reconciliation. In the Sacrament of Reconciliation, we tell God we are sorry for what we have done. We promise to do our best not to do it again. And we ask God's help in changing our ways. What a blessing to know that when we receive this sacrament our sins are not only forgiven but also forgotten.

The Man Who
Made Trouble

A long, long time ago, there lived a man named Saul. He lived in Jerusalem when the Church was just beginning. Saul did not believe that Jesus had risen from the dead. He did not believe that Jesus was the Messiah. He thought that the followers of Jesus were being disrespectful to God when they preached the Good News. Saul wanted to get rid of all of Jesus' friends.

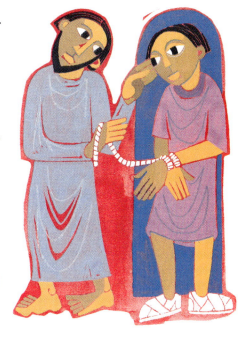

Saul worked for the Council of Jerusalem. His job was to make trouble for the early Christians. Saul went from house to house, arresting the men and women who believed in Jesus. Saul worked as hard as he could to get rid of all the Christians in the city. The followers of Jesus were afraid of Saul. Everyone except the apostles ran away to the country.

When Saul had arrested or chased almost all of the Christians out of Jerusalem, he went back to the Council. "I have done such a good job," he said. "Let me go to Damascus and get rid of the Jesus followers who live there. I'll find them all and put them in jail." The Council gave him permission, and off Saul went.

Damascus was a long way from Jerusalem. Saul traveled for days and days. "I'll show those troublemakers," thought Saul. "Those Jesus followers will not have a chance to escape." Saul could not wait to get to Damascus.

Then something absolutely amazing happened. When Saul was just outside the city, a great, blazing light came shooting down from heaven! Before he knew what happened, Saul found himself flat on the ground. He was surrounded by the light.

As Saul lay in the middle of the road he heard a voice. "Saul, Saul, why are you persecuting me?" the voice said.

Saul was really afraid. "Who are you?" he asked.

"I am Jesus, and you are persecuting me," the voice answered. "Get up now and go into the city. You will be told what to do."

Saul got up from the ground. He felt sick. He rubbed his eyes. He blinked and squinted. He opened his eyes as wide as he could. But Saul could not see. He was blind.

The men who were with Saul took him by the hand. They led him into the city. For three days Saul could not eat or drink anything. Saul knew that it was Jesus who had spoken to him. "What they are saying must be true," Saul thought. "This Jesus who was crucified is somehow still alive. He has beaten death. He must surely be the Messiah."

Saul prayed and prayed. He must have felt very sorry for hurting so many of Jesus' friends. Finally, on the third day, Saul had a visitor.

Saul's visitor was a man named Ananias. Ananias was a follower of Jesus. Jesus had spoken to Ananias in a vision. Jesus told him that he was to go to a certain house on Straight Street. Jesus said, "When you get there you will find a man called Saul. I want you to put your hands on him so that he can see again."

Ananias was afraid. He had heard all about Saul. "Lord," Ananias said, "people have told me about this man named Saul. He has come to our city to make trouble for your followers. If I go there he will arrest me."

Jesus said to Ananias, "I know you are afraid, but you still must go. I have big plans for Saul. He is going to help people from all over the world to know me." So Ananias went to Straight Street.

As soon as Ananias entered the house, he went up to Saul. He put his hands on Saul and said, "Brother Saul, I have been sent by Jesus, who appeared to you on your way here. I have been sent so that you can see again. I have been sent so that you may receive the Holy Spirit."

At that very second Saul could see again. He was baptized there and then. After he ate a little food, Saul began to feel strong again. In a few days, Saul began to preach. "Jesus is the Son of God," he said to anyone who would listen.

God forgave Saul, who had spent so much time making trouble for Jesus' friends. And Saul went on to become one of Jesus' best disciples. As Saul began to preach in other parts of the world people began to call him by his Roman name, Paul. He traveled everywhere telling people his story. He would tell them how good and forgiving God was. He would tell them about Jesus, who had died and risen from the dead. Paul would tell everyone he met all about the Good News.

God called Paul. Paul listened and answered. The great and Holy Spirit was not just with Paul, the Spirit was also in Paul. Paul let the Spirit move him and great things happened.

The Soldier Who Had No Enemies

Not so very long ago, there lived a very brave man named Maximilian Kolbe. Maximilian was a Franciscan priest. He lived in Poland during the Second World War. It was a very dangerous time to live. The Nazis were in power. They were very cruel. They arrested people and had them killed just because they were different. They also arrested people who spoke against their cruelty. That is how Maximilian ended up in prison. Maximilian had the courage to stand up to the evil that was taking over his country.

Maximilian grew up in an average Polish family. He had a loving mother and father and four brothers. Maximilian loved Jesus very much. He also had a special place in his heart for Jesus' mother, Mary. When he was a youngster, Maximilian thought about becoming a soldier. But when he grew up he did not join the regular army. Instead he became a soldier for

Mary. He wanted to help Mary win the hearts of all people. His weapons were words and love.

Maximilian started a magazine. In the magazine he wrote stories about the goodness of Jesus and the gentle love of Mary. He wanted everyone to know the Good News. And that is what he wrote about in his magazine.

Maximilian's magazine became very popular. Pretty soon he traveled to Japan to work with the people there. Maximilian loved the people of Japan.

Maximilian loved everyone. He believed there was good in all people.

Maximilian returned to Poland. He began to write for the magazine again. But his country had changed while he was away. Now the Nazis were in charge. Maximilian watched as people were beaten in the streets. He watched as all sorts of people were taken from their homes, arrested and sent away.

The Nazis especially hated the Jewish people. They arrested men, women and children and sent them to prisons. In the prisons the people got very little food or water. They had to work very hard. Those who became too weak to work anymore were killed. Almost all of the Jewish people who were sent to the prisons died.

Maximilian could not just sit back and watch what was happening. He knew evil when he saw it. What was happening was totally against the Plan of God. And so he began to write against what the Nazis were doing.

Twice he was arrested. The second time he was sent to Auschwitz. Auschwitz was one of the worst prisons. Now Maximilian had a new way of being a soldier for Mary. His courage and love touched many people.

When people were afraid, he sat with them. He spoke gentle, encouraging words about God's love. He secretly celebrated Mass with the other Catholics. Maximilian saved the small pieces of bread he received for his supper. This bread he blessed and shared. This bread became the Body and Blood of Jesus. Even in this dark, dingy, scary place the Church gathered and prayed together.

Often prisoners came to Maximilian and asked if they could receive the Sacrament of Penance. Maximilian heard their confessions. Then he asked a question: "Will you forgive those who have trespassed against you?" He was asking them to forgive even the cruel guards who hurt them. "Remember," he would say, "how Jesus forgave the people who put him to death on the cross." Maximilian never judged and his example helped others to forgive.

One day all of the prisoners were called out into the yard. They had to line up in straight rows. They were not allowed to speak. "A prisoner has escaped," the commander said. "You all know what that means. Ten of you will have to die to pay for his mistake."

The commander began to walk up and down the lines. Sometimes he stopped in front of a man. "You," he said, "step over there." And the man knew that he was one of the ten who was about to die.

When all ten men had been chosen, the commander began to look them up and down. One of the men began to weep. "Please," he said, "I have a wife and children. Please do not kill me. My family needs me." The soldier laughed at the crying man.

Without anyone noticing, Maximilian left his place in line. He began to walk to the front. He stood in front of the commander. "I would like to make a request," he said. The commander was curious about this man. "Well," he said, "what do you want?"

"I would like to take this man's place," Maximilian said. "I have no wife or children. I am weak. This man is healthier. He is a stronger worker." The soldier looked at Maximilian. "Who are you?" he asked. "I am a Catholic priest," Maximilian said. "Request granted," the commander replied. And he ordered the guards to march Maximilian and the other nine men away.

They were taken to a small hut and locked in. They were left there to starve to death. After two weeks the other nine men were dead, but Maximilian was still alive. The commander ordered that he be given a

poisonous shot. And that is what they did. Maximilian died. He gave up his life for another.

After the war was over, the people who had been with Maximilian in prison told stories of his bravery. They also remembered how loving and forgiving a person he was.

God called to Maximilian. Maximilian listened and answered. The great and Holy Spirit was not just with Maximilian, the Spirit was also in him. Maximilian let the Spirit move him and great things happened. In that dark and ugly prison, Maximilian was able to bring the joy and hope of God's Good News. He was even able to forgive those who were hurting him.

Spirit of Action

Jesus came to tell the world the Good News. Do you remember the Good News? It is that God loves everyone. And it is that God will always be with us. With the help of the Spirit it is now our job to tell the Good News.

Jesus also came to tell the world that it was time for the Plan of God to happen. Do you remember what the Plan of God is? It is that everyone will love God more than anything else and love others as they love themselves. With the help of the Spirit, it is now our job to help make the Plan of God happen.

It is not enough just to tell people the Good News. We also have to work to make the Plan of God come true. This means we feed the hungry and take care of the sick. It means we give water to the thirsty and clothes to people who need them. It means we will visit people who are sick or in prison.

This is the job of every Christian, but it is also the job of our whole Church. When someone is working alone, it is easy to get worn out and discouraged. It is much easier when we work with each other and with the Holy Spirit. We can encourage each other. We can help each other. This is where we find the Holy Spirit, where the Church is acting together. When we let the Holy Spirit move us, great things happen.

We receive the gift of the Holy Spirit when we are baptized. The gifts of the Spirit are increased when we receive the Sacrament of Confirmation. Through this special sign, the whole Church celebrates that God is with us and we are with God. We celebrate God as a Spirit of action.

A Letter
of Good News

A long, long time ago, there lived a man named James. James was the leader of the Church in Jerusalem. It was an exciting time to be a Christian. Peter and Paul and some of the other disciples were traveling all over the world telling people about Jesus. James, who was not one of the twelve apostles, got to stay home and help take care of all of the Jewish Christians.

James's job was to make sure that the followers of Jesus did not forget what Jesus taught. James knew that Jesus had come to tell people the Good News. James wanted the people to remember that they were also supposed to share the Good News.

This is the Good News: God loves everyone very much, and it is time to make the Plan of God happen. Everyone and everything in the world was supposed to live in peace and harmony. People were supposed to love God with their whole hearts and love their neighbors as themselves. James had a very important job.

Sometimes when James walked through the city, he saw things that he did not like. He saw people with gold rings on their fingers and people who wore shabby clothes being treated differently. "You should treat everyone the same," he said. "You should not give rich people the best places to sit and make poor people sit on the floor."

Sometimes he saw the followers of Jesus not behaving as they should. "Why are you fighting with each other?" he asked. "Maybe it is because you want something that you do not even need. Do not let the world tell you what you must have. Remember, if you pray, God will give you everything that you really need."

One day James was talking to one of his helpers. "I am very concerned," James said. "Some people say they believe in Jesus, but they do not act like they believe in the Good News. They have forgotten about the Plan of God. They have forgotten that God wants peace and harmony for the world. They have forgotten that they have to make the Plan of God happen."

"I think I will write them a letter," he said. "I will remind them that they cannot say they love God with

their whole hearts if they do not love their neighbors as themselves. They must help out the widows and the orphans. They must make sure that everyone has enough clothes to wear and food to eat. I will write them a letter to remind them what it means to be a disciple of Jesus." And so James wrote an epistle, or letter, to all the believers.

James was a good leader. He reminded the people that it was not enough to just say, "I believe in Jesus." James told the people, "You will know the real followers of Jesus not just by what they say but also by the way they act."

James was a great disciple of Jesus. He shared the Good News. He worked hard to make the Plan of God happen. James's letter is still reminding people that if the Plan of God is to happen, they will have to get busy.

God called James. James listened and answered. The great and Holy Spirit was not just with James; the Spirit was also in James. James let the Spirit move him and great things happened.

The Bishop for the Poor

Not so very long ago, there lived a holy man who was not only kind but also very brave. This man was one of the leaders of our Church. He was an archbishop. This brave, holy man's name was Oscar Romero. Oscar Romero was archbishop of a country called El Salvador.

El Salvador is in Central America. It is a beautiful land, but it has many problems. For many years, all of the land was owned by a few rich families. Almost all of the people who lived in El Salvador worked for these families. Even though people worked very hard, they were paid very little. They were very poor and were treated badly. The government and the police were on the side of the rich families. Sometimes people were even murdered if they caused trouble for these families.

When Oscar Romero became the archbishop, the rich people were happy. "He will stay out of our way," they said. "He will not cause us any trouble. He will stay busy with his learning and his reading." And they were right. During Oscar's first years as archbishop he decided he would not take sides. He would just pay attention to Church business. He would leave the government alone. Then one day his good friend, Father Grande, was murdered.

Father Grande had been working with the poor people of El Salvador. He saw how much they suffered. He saw how mean the soldiers were. He saw how people were tortured and murdered if they spoke against the unfair way they were treated. Father Grande said, "This is not right. God wants freedom and justice for all people. God wants peace and harmony, but God does not want rich people to make poor people suffer."

Father Grande spoke against the rich families and the government for the way they were acting.

One day when Father Grande was riding in a jeep, some soldiers stopped him. The soldiers shot and killed Father Grande. They shot and killed the old man who was with him. They shot and killed the teenager who was with him, too. Father Grande, the old man and the teenager joined the list of thousands who had been murdered because they spoke up for freedom and justice in El Salvador.

Father Grande's body was carried to the cathedral. (A cathedral is the main church in a city. It is where the bishop or archbishop preaches and says Mass.) Archbishop Romero was very sad. He knew his friend was a good man. "This should not have happened," he thought. "Father Grande wanted only what God wanted for all people: freedom and justice." For a very long time, the archbishop thought and prayed. He thought and prayed and then prayed even more. The archbishop spent hours and hours praying.

At that very moment God was calling Oscar Romero. Oscar Romero listened and he answered. The Spirit was not only with the archbishop, the Spirit was also in him. Oscar Romero let the Spirit move him, and the lives of thousands of people were changed forever. Oscar Romero became a hero. He

took up his cross just as Jesus had done. And, like Jesus, Oscar carried the cross to his death. Oscar Romero's cross was the unjust treatment of the people of El Salvador.

From that day on, Archbishop Romero began to speak up for the poor. He told his priests to protect the poor. He began programs to help fix the problems in his country. He knew that if the Plan of God was going to happen in El Salvador, he could no longer be silent. He even told the soldiers, "These are your brothers and sisters you are killing. In the name of God, you must stop."

The rich people who used to have supper with Oscar no longer spoke to him. The government leaders told him they could not promise him safety. The archbishop was very smart. He knew that the people in power were going to try to quiet him. He knew that if he did not stop speaking out against the evil of injustice, he would probably be killed like his friend Father Grande. The archbishop was ready to die for what he believed. He was ready to die just like the Lord he loved so much, Jesus.

And that is what happened. On March 24, 1980, Archbishop Oscar Romero was murdered. He was

shot to death while he was celebrating Mass. He died because he wanted to make the Plan of God happen. He wanted peace and justice for the people of his land. Oscar Romero was a martyr. Martyrs are people who die for what they believe in. Archbishop Oscar Romero believed in the Good News for all people. He was a holy, kind and very brave man.

God called the archbishop. The archbishop listened and answered. The great and Holy Spirit was not just with the archbishop; the Holy Spirit was in him. Archbishop Oscar Romero let the Spirit move him and great things happened. The world is a better place because of Oscar Romero. He stood up for his beliefs. He helped the poor. He comforted the sorrowful. He took care of the sick. He helped make the Plan of God happen.

The Spirit has great gifts to give us: patience, courage, joy, wisdom. All we need to do is be open to the Spirit. If we let the Spirit move, we will have the Spirit's power. We can help to make the Plan of God happen in our own homes, in our schools and in our communities.

The Not-the-End

Stories, stories, stories—we have read a lot of stories. We have heard about all sorts of people who lived at different times and grew up in different lands. They all had their own stories. But they were each a part of a much larger story.

It is a story that began when the earth was brand new. It is a story that began when God first called out to Adam and Eve, and Adam and Eve sang and danced their answer. From before there was time, God has called out. And people have answered.

Now God is calling you. God is calling you by name. There is no one else in the whole world like you. There has never been anyone like you since before time began. No one else can do what God is calling you to do. You are a part of God's story.

Your story is just beginning. There are all sorts of wonderful surprises ahead. Just remember, the great and Holy Spirit is with you and in you. If you let the Spirit move you, great things will happen.

The Spirit Is With You

Write your name or the appropriate pronoun (his/her, he/she) on the dotted lines below. Fill in the rest of the story. Ask an adult for help where you need it.

Today, this very day, there lives a young person

named ....

.... is _____ years old

and lives in _____.

.... lives with

_____.

....'s best friend's name is

_____.

They like to spend their free time _____

_____.

.... knows that God

loves .... very much. Sometimes

.... likes to talk to God.

This is what .... tells God.

_____

_____.

One of ....'s favorite stories

about Jesus is _____

_____

_____ .

When .... grows up,

.... would like to

_____

_____

_____ .

God called .... and

.... listened and answered.

The great and Holy Spirit is not just with

....

but also in ....

When ....lets the Spirit

move ...., great things happen.

This is one of the ways ....

would like to help make the Plan of God happen.

_____

_____

_____

_____

_____

_____

_____ .